HARRY HAMMER

Book Two:
Shark Star

D0510173

With thanks to Paul Ebbs

A TEMPLAR BOOK

First published in the UK in 2013 by Templar Publishing,
an imprint of The Templar Company Limited,
Deepdene Lodge, Deepdene Avenue,
Dorking, Surrey, RH5 4AT, UK

www.templarco.co.uk

Text and concept copyright © 2013 by Hothouse Fiction
Illustration copyright © 2013 by Aaron Blecha

First edition

All rights reserved

ISBN 978-1-84877-733-0

Printed and bound by CPI Group (UK) Ltd,
Croydon, CR0 4YY

HARRY HAMMER

Shark Star

by DAVY OCEAN

Illustrated by Aaron Blecha

templar

Chapter 1

"Open wider!" Ralph yells.

"Ahh caaaaaannn't!" I splutter.

"Open wider!"

"Ahh said, ahh caaaaaannn't!"

"What?"

"Ghet zout ov muh mouf!"

Ralph swims out of my mouth and frowns

at me. "Harry, I can't understand what you're saying. Why are you speaking in code?"

Now Ralph is out of my mouth I can speak properly again. "I can't open my mouth wider!" I say. "If you went in any further you'd be able to shake fins with my bum!"

It's the first day of the half-term holiday and me and my best friends Joe and Ralph are supposed to be on our way to Shark Park. We're supposed to be on our way to Shark Park, but Joe has made us stop so he can go into KOIs R US for the latest set of koi carp cards, and Ralph has taken the opportunity for a feed.

Ralph narrows his eyes. "How else am I supposed to get my breakfast? I'm a pilot fish, and pilot fish eat the leftover food from between sharks' teeth. It's how we've always done it and I don't see why we should change now."

"I'm not saying we should change it.

I just don't want to swallow you!"

Ralph flicks his tail crossly. "Well if you'd saved me some of your prawn-flakes in your front teeth, maybe I wouldn't have to go searching the back of your mouth for bits of last night's tea."

I poke about at the back of my mouth with my tongue and flip out two pieces of yesterday's clamburger. Ralph gobbles them up greedily, then floats in front of me, looking hopeful.

"That's all there is," I say, as Joe swims out of the shop empty tentacled. "They haven't got the new cards in till tomorrow," Joe says miserably.

"Well, I'm going to need something else to stop my tummy rumbling," Ralph moans. "Half a prawn-flake and two smidges of clamburger aren't enough for a growing pilot fish."

Ralph and Joe swim off towards Shark Park. I hope they cheer up before we get there. Holidays are supposed to be fun, but they're not if your best mates are mooning around like a couple of bluefish.

As we get to the park gates Joe turns to me. "Do we have to go in?" he asks gloomily. "I still haven't recovered from what happened last time."

Ralph starts to snigger at the

memory and, I have to admit, it was pretty funny. What happened last time was this:

1. Joe jumped on the Wrecked-Ship's-Wheel roundabout, but he hadn't realised how fast it was going.

2. He came flying off.

3. He shot right up the Slime-Algae-Slide THE WRONG WAY...

4. He catapulted around the Whale-Rib-Swings SIXTEEN times, and then...

5. He landed with a huge TWANG on the Seahorse-on-a-Spring...

6. Which BOINGED him right up towards the surface of the sea like an out-of-control jellycopter!

If it hadn't been for me and Ralph
swimming up as fast as we could to catch
him, Joe would have plopped right out
into the air. And everyone knows how
bad being in the air is for a jellyfish, the
heat of the sun can turn them crispy in
seconds.

Joe eyes the sign by the gate
suspiciously. The sign says "SHARK PARK
– FAMILY FUN FOR EVERYONE!"

"Hmm, I don't call being spun
around like my mum's washing fun,"
Joe mutters. "I don't call being thrown
through the water upside down fun!"

I decide not to tell Joe that

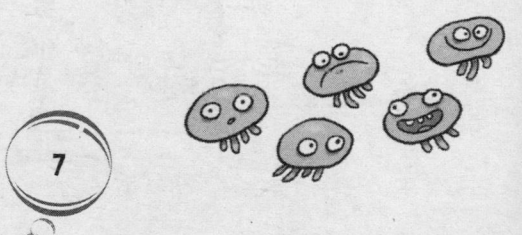

watching him get flung around the park
was fun for me and Ralph.

   I look around Shark Park – at the
roundabout, the slide, the swings and the
seahorse – and then I look
at Joe, who is folding

each of his arms over the other. One
by one. This is going to take a very long
time, so I hold up a fin. "Okay, okay," I say,
"we'll do something else."

To be honest, I don't know why I suggested shark park in the first place. It's half-term for all the kids in Shark Point, not just us three. That means the place is stuffed to the gills with fish and sharks and dolphins and octopi. So I turn back to Ralph and Joe. "It's already full," I say. "It'll be ages before we can get on the Whale-Rib-Swings and they're the best thing in the park." Ralph and Joe nod, so I carry on. "We're all too old to go on the Seahorse-on-a-Spring." Ralph nods. Joe hides behind Ralph and his bottom pops. I know he's trying to be brave but the Seahorse TWANGING

incident did scare him quite a bit. "The only thing left for us to do would be to go and play on the sea-grass, but loads of girl-fish—"

"Yuck," say Joe and Ralph together at the mention of girls.

'—are playing flounders." (Flounders is like rounders but you hit a sea urchin with a bat made from a swordfish-nose.)

I don't tell Ralph and Joe my last reason for wanting to leave, because I don't want to look like a scaredy-catfish. Rick Reef and Donny Dogfish are bound to be in Shark Park today, and I really don't want to swim into them. Rick is a

reef shark in our class at school and his favourite subject is trying to annoy me. He does very well at it. In fact, you could say he is a grade A student when it comes to making fun of hammerheads.

Ralph and Joe nod in agreement.

"Staying in Shark Park is going to be boring," says Ralph.

"And probably deadly," Joe adds grimly. So we turn around, and head back into Shark Point.

The town is swarming with kids too – all just as bored as us.

We fin our way down the main street. There are complaining fish being dragged into shops by their mums, and a bunch of hard-looking scallops hanging out on the corner of Coral Drive. They're trying to be cool by blowing farts out of the side of their shell in tune to the music coming out of the Amusement Arcade. The three of us swim past them pretty quickly, hoping not to catch their eye.

As I watch a kid dolphin being told off by his grumpy looking dad I realise that it could be a lot worse. At least I'm able to hang out with my friends. At least I'm not being dragged around town by my dad. Luckily, my dad is Mayor of Shark Point so he hardly ever gets any time off. Which means I never have to be dragged around by him in the holidays. I can't imagine anything worse.

Except.

"Harrrrrrrrrrrrrrrrrrrrrrrrrrrrrry!"

Suddenly I can.

Oh no!

It's Mum! She's swimming as fast

as she can towards us. "I thought you
boys were going to Shark Park," she says
as she reaches us, taking a large, spotty
handkerchief from her finbag and wiping
something off my lip.

"Bogey," she whispers. But she
might as well have
shouted it. Ralph and
Joe both heard
and they're
laughing so
hard behind
their fins and
tentacles I think
they might choke.

Mum then makes it even worse by grabbing my fin and pulling me away. "Well seeing as you're not in the park, you can come with me to see your dad opening the leisure centre."

My tummy sinks twenty fathoms and I try to pull away, but Mum is holding me too tight. All I can see ahead is Mum pulling me along, and all I can hear behind is Ralph and Joe giggling.

Mum and Dad always want me to come and see him opening stuff, and making speeches. Usually I can find a way out of it, but not this time. I so wish we'd stayed in Shark Park!

We turn a corner on to Starfish Square, and I see a huge crowd of fish and squids cheering outside the gleaming new Shark Point Leisure Centre. There is a flag billowing from the roof and banners hung above the door. Click! Click! Click! Electric eel photographers flash their electric eel tail flashguns at the doors of the leisure centre as my dad proudly swims to the front of the crowd.

He waves his fin and taps his nose on the waiting microphone to make sure it's working.

Mum finally lets go of me so she can clap her fins and whistle at Dad. Seriously, I don't know where to look. I can feel my cheeks start to go red as Ralph and Joe look at me and back to Dad. Dad is a popular mayor, but he can be really embarrassing sometimes. Ralph and Joe know this and I can see they're waiting for him to say or do something stupid so they can pull my fin about it for the rest of the week.

Mum just keeps waving at Dad and

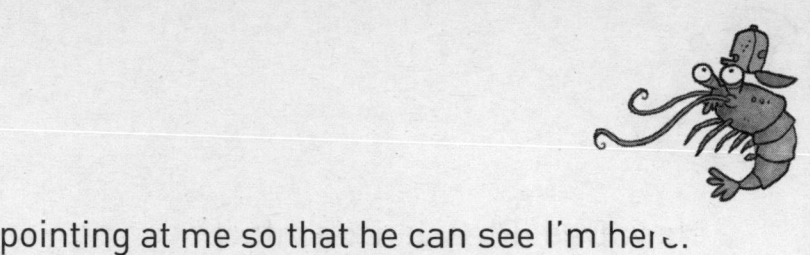

pointing at me so that he can see I'm here.

Dad waves back enthusiastically, and the eels all turn their cameras on me! I can feel myself going redder than the reddest red snapper as Mum throws her fin round me and tells me to "smiley-wile." That's when Ralph and Joe fall over backwards and almost die from laughing. This is the worst thing EVER!

"Yes, right, well – hullo!" shouts Dad in his usual absent-minded way. "Right, yes, well, I would like to welcome you all here today..."

Don't do it!

"But before we begin..."

Dad. Please. Don't do it!

"I'd just like to say that seeing you all here has reminded me..."

Nope. He's going to do it. He's going to tell one of his awful jokes. I try to hide under Ralph and Joe.

"Why did the deaf pirate come to hear my speech today?"

Silence.

"Because," and here Dad chuckles to himself, "because he thought I was going to be opening a Treasure Centre!"

No one laughs apart from Mum. But Dad doesn't realise that his joke has gone down quicker than the Titanic and just

carries on as if nothing has happened.
"So I duly declare the Shark Point Leisure
Centre o—"

A piece of yellow seaweed drifts
towards Dad's face and catches him
in the eye. As he raises a fin to wipe it
away, he accidentally slices the 'Opening
Today!' ribbon that's stretched across the
doors. Before he has a chance to say,
"—pen!", he is bounced out of the way by
the rushing crowd and sent spinning up
to the roof of the leisure centre, where
he gets tangled in the flag and stuck to
the flagpole!

I watch in horror as the

photographers focus their cameras on Dad. Mum squeals and swims up to try and untangle him from the flagpole, as the cameras flash and flash and flash.

I know what's going to be on the front page of the *Seaweed Times* tomorrow – my Dad wrapped around the flagpole like a shark kebab. And that means everyone in Shark Point is going to be laughing at him.

And laughing at me for having such an embarrassing dad!

I pull Joe and Ralph away.

I have to pull them because they've been laughing so much they've forgotten how to swim.

It's not until we're all the way on the other side of town by the cinema that their laughing stops. And finally I see something that cheers me up. Outside the cinema is a huge poster of Gregor the Gnasher's first film, Parrotfish of the Caribbean, in which he plays Captain Jack Spratt, the all-action hero. In the poster he's wrestling with a giant squid.

GREGOR THE GNASHER

PARROTFISH OF THE CARIBBEAN

Gregor is my total hero. Mum calls him 'that tooth head', but she doesn't understand – he's the Underwater Wrestling Champion of the World and now he's started making films.

He's a total legend. It must be so cool to be a famous great white. I bet Gregor's kids don't ever get embarrassed by him.

I would have said, "let's go and see

the film!" but I've not had my pocket-money yet, and with Dad currently stuck on the roof of the leisure centre, it wasn't about to happen any time soon. So we carry on swimming until eventually, with nowhere else to go, and nothing else to do, we end up outside the library.

"The library?" says Ralph. "Talk about double boring."

"Well, what else can we do?" I say.

Thankfully, Joe comes to my rescue. "It's probably the safest place to go," he says. "Unless, of course, a bookcase falls on our heads."

I slap a fin across my face. It would

be less work to be in school! But I lead them both inside anyway.

At least there's no chance of running into Rick and Donny in the library. Rick's only interest in books is how hard he can throw them at my hammerhead when Mrs Shelby isn't looking.

So now we're sitting bored in the silent library, too bored to even pick up a book.

"Is it lunch time yet?" Ralph whispers, looking at my teeth.

"The edges of those books look quite sharp," Joe mumbles, twiddling his

tentacles nervously. "I think we'd better just sit here and not move."

Great. It's the first day of the holiday and we're stuck in the library doing impressions of rocks.

I sigh, and try and think of something cool to do in silence that doesn't involve moving.

When...

"Wooooooooooooooooooooooooooooo ooooooooooooooooooooo!!!"

The shriek splits the quiet, and I spin around in my chair, expecting to see Rick Reef waving a spider-crab in front of a kid squid or something. But it's not,

it's Pearl and Cora, the dolphin twins.
They're dancing round and round, high-
finning and shrieking, looking at their
aqua-phones, looking at each other, then
looking back at their aqua-phones, then
looking at each other
and...

"Wooooooooo
ooooooooooo
ooooooooooo
oooooooooo
ooooooooo!!!"
-ing again.
The
librarian, Mr

Gape, an elderly basking shark, heaves himself out of his chair and swims over to Pearl and Cora. "Will you two please be quiet? This is a library, not a fairground!"

"But—" says Pearl.

"There's—" says Cora.

Mr Gape holds up a huge fin to shush them. "Not another word, or I must ask you to leave."

"We were leaving anyway," says Pearl.

"Oh really?" says Mr Gape.

"Yes," says Cora. "We've got somewhere way more interesting to go than this boring old library!"

"And what, may I ask, could be more interesting than a library?" Mr Gape bellows, causing several people to drop their books in shock.

"Something," Pearl says, her voice rising towards another shriek, "that we've just seen on the interwet!"

"What?" demands Mr Gape.

"Leggy air-breathers! They've been spotted just off Shark Point and they're

making a FILM! Woooooooooooooooooo
ooooooooooooooooooooooooooo!!!" Pearl
and Cora rush past us, spinning Joe
round three times and knocking me and
Ralph flat in their wake.

But I don't care about getting
knocked over. I have too many things on
my mind.

1. A film?
2. A film????
3. (And every OTHER number!) A FILM????

This half-term just got interesting!!!!

Chapter 2

"Let's go," I say the minute Pearl
and Cora leave the building.

Joe looks at me and frowns. "I want
to stay here with the nice safe books!"

I look at Ralph. "Who wants to see
a film being made?" he says feebly. "I
don't, films are like books that move, and

we know how boring books are. I think I'd
rather stay here with all the... books..."
His voice trails off, not being able to think
of any more rubbish reasons not to leave
the library. Ralph's been afraid of leggy
air-breathers ever since he accidentally
got caught in one of their nets.

"We'll just go and have a look,
okay?" I say. "We won't go anywhere near
the leggies, I promise. Cross my swim
bladder and hope to fry."

Ralph isn't convinced, but I'm
desperate to get after Cora and Pearl. "I
will keep you both totally and utterly and
completely safe."

"Do you promise?" says Joe.

I nod my hammerhead – and nearly knock Mr Gape over. "I promise. And afterwards I'll go and get something to eat," I add, looking at Ralph.

Ralph's eyes glaze over, hungrily. "Will you get sardine nuggets?"

I nod.

"With a portion of sprats?"

"Yes. With a portion of sprats."

"A super-sized portion of sprats?"

"Yes!" I say impatiently. If we don't get going we'll never catch up with Pearl and Cora.

"All right then," says Ralph

reluctantly.

"All right then," says Joe, even more reluctantly.

But I don't care how reluctant they are – they've said yes and that's all that counts.

And now we're going to see a film being made. A FILM! How cool is that? My heart leaps like a bar of soap from wet fins at the thought!

I speed down the street, refusing to let go of Joe. Ralph is doing his best to keep up, but because he's quite a little fish he can't kick as hard as me, so I wrap my free fin around him, and let him

hitch a lift as I kick and kick and kick.

"But the leggies," yells Joe. "What if they catch us and eat us... or worse?"

"They're making a film," I say, "not trying to catch us and eat us."

"But what if they're making a film ABOUT catching and eating us?" whines Joe.

He might have a point there, but I don't want him to know that. So I change the subject. "What if Gregor the Gnasher is there? What if he's the star?"

I think back to the poster for Parrotfish of the Caribbean and the picture of Gregor wrestling with the giant evil squid. I wonder what it must be like to actually be in a movie. I imagine that it's me up there on the poster and that I'm a world-famous movie star who lives in a huge house in Driftywood (where all the famous movie stars work and live). I start to grin as I picture being fed peeled shrimp twenty-four hours a day by my butlers, Rick Reef and Donny Dogfish!

But then it all goes wrong.

Suddenly, on the poster, the giant squid has grabbed me by the tail and he's using my hammerhead to bang nails into the side of a ship! My face starts to go red, and I feel stupid for even dreaming that I could ever be cool enough to be a movie star. Thankfully I forget about my hammerhead once the huge, dark, open ocean approaches and we

leave Shark Point behind. I can see
the sunlight glinting on the tops of
the waves. The beautiful yellow light
shimmers in time with the pops coming
from Joe's bottom as he gets more and
more frightened. I look down at him and
he goes red, then blue and then even
yellower than normal.

Jellyfish do that when they're
scared.

In the distance, Cora and Pearl are
swimming as fast as they can. Normally
I'm one of the fastest swimmers around,
but with Ralph and Joe slowing me down
I'm finding it hard to keep up. Pearl and

Cora are not only swimming around each other and high-finning when they come close, but they're also double-ending and tail-swapping as they go.

Up ahead I can see the shadow of a boat bobbing and skipping on the waves. As I look closer I can see a brighter light than the sun shining in the sea. There's a leggie dangling in the water, dressed in a rubbery wetsuit. She's holding a massive light and swinging it around like the lighthouse on the shore above Shark Point.

SPLOSH!!!

Another leggie

crashes into the water and I can see he's holding a camera. He's moving about, all excited, and pointing to the light-holding leggie. He wants her to shine the light over towards me!

My heart starts to pound. I let go of Ralph and Joe, smooth down my hammer with my fin and give my best sharky grin.

The light shines right in my eyes and I strike a pose – just as heroic as Gregor in the poster, if a little hammer-ier.

But then it goes dark again as the light in my eyes moves away.

I look about, wondering what's going on. Here I am, all ready for them, but they're pointing their camera and light in completely the wrong direction!

And then I see what's happened.

My heart sinks like an anchor.

There, in the spotlight, flexing his fin muscles and pointing his tail, is Rick Reef! He's triple-nosing from the slickest fin slide into the über-coolest gill slam I have ever seen. Even I have to admit it is pretty amazing, and I feel the bottom fall out of my world.

Just as the world falls out of Joe's bottom.

"Sorry!" he says.

"Shh!" I hiss at him. Rick finishes on an old-skool reverse dorsal, spins on his tail and throws his fins wide.

Not only are the leggies following Rick's every move with the camera, but Cora and Pearl are screaming, "Rick! Rick! Rick!" in their best cheerleader voices.

"Suppose we'd better go then," says Ralph gloomily. "No one's gonna want to film us if we're up against Rick."

I hold up my fin. "Not so fast. I

haven't even started yet. There's no way I'm going to let Rick have all the limelight. He's not the only shark in Shark Point!"

I kick away from Ralph and Joe until I am right under the shadow of the boat.

That's when Rick notices me.

He keeps smiling and waving to the camera with his fin, but under his breath, he says, "Swim on home anchor-face, they're not here to film a freak show. They want real sharks, like me."

I grit my teeth and flip into a double-endy.

"Harry!" calls Joe, "be careful! That boat has propellers. You don't want to end up getting liquidised!"

Rick laughs. "See. Even your mates think you're a clumsy dork."

In the background, I can hear Donny Dogfish, Rick's sidekick, laughing behind his fin. I glare at him, trying to look tough, but it just makes me go cross-eyed and he laughs even more.

Cora and Pearl are still chanting and suddenly I feel really annoyed. I'll show those dolphins, Rick and most importantly the leggies exactly what a hammerhead can do.

I push past Rick right into the camera light. Curling up my tail and taking a deep breath, I begin.

This is what happens:

1. I do a perfect nose stall.
2. Rick sniggers and busts three gill slams.
3. Gritting my teeth harder, I swoosh a double inside-outy.
4. Rick shouts, "Easy!" Then he does exactly the same thing and finishes on an almost impossible outside-inny!
5. I race towards the boat's shadow and curl a wicked single flip.
6. Joe is shouting at me to calm down, but I'm

not listening.

7. Rick is right behind me, doing a full-on eye-closed belly rush!

8. Joe screams something about me getting too close to the boat.

9. I yell at Joe to shut up and fall backwards into a desperate upside-down devil smash.

10. I can see that the leggies love it. They are swinging their light this way and that, following me and Rick with the camera.

11. Rick starts whizzing in ever tighter circles. I can't believe what Rick is planning to do... He wouldn't! He couldn't!

Rick does! I don't believe it!

He bursts out of the middle of a swirl of bubbles and heads straight towards the surface. I can see him looking back at me with big crazy eyes, as he kicks with his tail as hard as he possibly can.

Cora and Pearl are yelling him on. Even Joe and Ralph are watching with their mouths agape, as Rick whoooooooooshes past the leggies and BREAKS THE SURFACE!!!!!!

Through the sparkling waves I can see
his shivering shadow twisting in the air
above the ocean. He does a graceful
double nose and tail touch, and then
SPLASHES back into
the water. The
leggies go
crazy.

That's it!

Spin. Kick. Spin. Kick. SPIN. KICK. SPIN! KICK!! SPIN!!! KICK!!!!

BANG!!!!!!!

I'm heading for the surface too. I'm going double... no, three... no, four times faster than Rick did. I'm heading up towards the sunlight with Pearl and Cora's screams and Joe's 'Nooooooooo oooooooooooooooooooooooooooooooo!!!' ringing in my ears.

SPLLLLLAAAAAAAAAAAAAAASH HHHHHHHHHHHHHHHH!!!!!I break the surface and I'm out into the air!

Flying higher and higher.

I know exactly the trick I want to bust. A triple-goofy gill slap and tail flip.

I twist and kick, still rising. Twisting. Turning. Feeling the wind on my sides, smelling the unfamiliar salty air, feeling the rush over my hammer as I ripple and twist.

I've done it! A full stunt above the waves, in mid-air with room to spare.

There's no way the cameras are still going to be on Rick.

I'm gonna be a STAR!!!!!

Well, I would have been a star if it hadn't been for the following six things...

1.   I'd come out of the water too fast.

2.   I'd pushed up too high.

3.   I hadn't thought about my re-entry after the tail-flip.

4.   And...

5.   And...

6.   Oh..

I crash down out of the sky and land with a wet, breathless slap – right on the deck of the boat!

SLAP!

Chapter 3

I don't know who's screaming louder, me
or the leggies. They're running in every
direction, waving their hands in the air in
panic. I'm on my front trying to flip myself
off the side, back into the water, and
realising that I can't breathe!

    This is bad. Proper bad.

If I had time and wasn't about to suffocate to death I'd slap myself around the head with my tail for being so stupid.

All I can see are running legs, and all I can feel is the hot sun on my back and it is starting to dry me out! I have to admit to myself that Joe was right, which makes the whole situation even worse.

I try yelling to the leggies to help me but all that comes out is a terrifying hiss that seems to scare them even more. A couple of them even look like they're about to throw themselves in the water to get away from me. I think they change their minds when they realise that there might be one shark on the boat, but there are hundreds in the ocean.

I manage to get one fin underneath me and lift my head a bit, so I can see a bit more of what's going on. I look around and see that most of the leggies are huddled at one end of the boat. There are two more leggies, a man and a lady, climbing out of the water. One of them puts down a camera and the other a huge light and they start waving their arms around. They're the filmmakers from the water!

I don't think this is the best time for me to show off, but I do try and give

them a smile.

The lady screams and the man leaps back and nearly falls back into the water. I close my mouth and frown. Why are they so scared? But once I have my mouth closed they get a little braver and start coming towards me with their hands

outstretched.

Slowly, I try to move forward using my fins and tail, but I just fall back on my belly with a slap. The two leggies coming towards me take a small step back, as if they expect me to bite them. I wish I could explain to them that I'm really not interested in eating them. I JUST WANT TO GET BACK IN THE WATER!!!

I look at them with each eye on the end of my hammer and try my best to lay still. The leggies look at each other, nod and start walking towards me again.

It's getting really difficult to breathe now and I'm finding it hard to stay calm.

The leggies grab hold of my fins and drag me to the side of the boat.

The wood of the deck tickles my belly and I let out a giggle, which comes out sounding a bit like an angry hiss. The leggies let go again and I have to think of something really sad to stop the giggling. I picture Rick posing on a movie poster. It makes me feel angry rather than sad, but

at least it stops me from laughing.

The leggies grab me again and take me right to the edge of the boat. I swivel my eyes around and see that the really scared leggies are getting a bit braver now. They edge closer to get a better look. The leggies heave me on to the side of the boat. I can see the ocean, all wet and inviting below me, and then the other leggies coming towards me.

A few of them are brave enough to give me a little stroke before I get pushed back into the water.

Thank Cod! I can breathe again!

But as the bubbles clear, all I can

hear is laughter.

Rick is right in my face, clutching his sides with his fins. Big, fat laughs are coming out of his mouth in huge snorts. Behind him, Cora and Pearl are laughing too. They have their fins across each other's shoulders and they are laughing so much I think they're going to be sick.

"There he goes!" calls Rick as I swim away as fast as I can. "The shark so clumsy he can't miss a tiny boat in the middle of the ocean! You want to get those hammerhead sensors seen to, Harry. They're obviously as rubbish as the rest of you!"

Red-faced, and with hot tears in my eyes, I swim and swim and swim. I can hear Ralph and Joe calling out to me but I don't care. I have to get out of here.

"How useless are hammerhead sharks?" Rick shouts after me. "A whole bunch of leggies to chew on and he lets them push him back into the sea. Me,

I'd love to eat a leggy air-breather if I got the chance. Not Harry though. Harry is their PET!"

I don't stop for anyone until I get home.

I can hear Mum in the kitchen. Dad probably won't be back from his office yet – or he's still trapped on the leisure centre roof – so I might be able to sneak in without anyone noticing.

But as I try and skulk past the kitchen, my catfish swims over and starts purring loudly.

"Is that you, angel-fish?" Mum calls

from the kitchen.

I hate it when she calls me that.

"No," I say. "It's The Most Rubbish Shark in the History of the Sea and the leggy air-breathers have it all on film to prove it!"

Mum comes out of the kitchen, wiping her fins on a tea towel. "What are you talking about?"

So I tell her.

When I finish, mum wraps her fins around me and cuddles me close.

I hate it when she does that as well.

Why can't she just leave me alone? Can't she see I want to go to my room

and sulk?

Mum wets the edge of her sea sponge with her tongue and wipes some seaweed from my face.

"Sounds like you've had a rotten day. Why don't I make you a lovely dinner and then you can have a soak in the hot spring and I'll give you a proper old skin-scrub, like I did when you were a baby? I have a really lovely new sea-urchin scrubber. You used to love that."

Could my day get any worse?

Well yes, it seems that it could.

Mum makes me sit in the kitchen while she cooks dinner. "As you're so

upset, I've made
you a whole plate
of leggie-
shaped fish cakes
and coral crunchies!
They'll make you all better."

My dinner is so babyish that not
even Ralph would be willing to clean it
from between my teeth.

Not that I care about Ralph any
more.

Or Joe.

I don't want to see anyone ever
again. I'm way too ashamed.

When Mum isn't looking, I pour the

leftovers out of the window and make it look like I've cleared my plate. Mum goes straight back to the cooker. "That's my hungry little starfish! I'll make you some more."

I hold up a fin. "No thanks Mum," I say. "That was lovely but I'm full and I'm tired. I think I just need to go to bed."

"What a sensible little starfish!" Mum beams. "How about I sing you a lullaby then? That always cheers you up." I open my mouth but it's too late. "Rock-a-bye, Harry, on the sea top," she shrieks.

Ahhhhhhhhh! Of all the lullabies in existence why did she have to pick the

one that mentions the sea-top?

"I've got to go, Mum," I say, swimming for the door. Mum blocks my way with her hammerhead and gives me a big, slobbery kiss. I close my eyes and wish that I was in a terrible nightmare. At least then I'd be able to wake up. But I'm not in a nightmare. Mum pats me on the hammerhead and finally lets me go. I swim to my bedroom so fast my stupid head gets jammed in the door.

Once I finally make it in, I slam the door
and throw myself on the bed.

What a rubbish, RUBBISH day!
I don't think I've ever been so
embarrassed. Not even when dad
accidentally tripped on Queen Aquae the
Third's robe and fell into her lap on LIVE
TELEVISION!

That's it, I think to myself, I'm not
going out again for this whole, entire
holiday. If I don't go out again I won't
see my dad making a fool of himself as
he tries to open stuff and make stupid
speeches and I won't bump into Rick and
the dolphin twins. And I won't be filmed

making a complete fool of myself.

Sorted.

There's tons I could be getting on with at home anyway. It won't be that bad to stay indoors for the holiday, will it? I mean, I'm a clever shark – I can find loads to do. I'll make a list to show you.

Right.

1. Umm, I could...
2. No wait, I know...
3. It might be a good idea if... no... right.
4. This is turning out to be a much harder list to make than I imagined.

Whatever.

I don't care if I'm so stupid and rubbish that I can't even make a list of what to do while I'm all stupid and rubbish!

5. I'm staying in my room for the whole holiday and that's that!

Chapter 4

Hmmmmmmmmmmm!

I don't want to open my eyes.

Hmmmmmmmmmm!! Hmmmmmmm!!

I'm not going to open my eyes. I snuggle deeper into my bed and flip more seaweed blankets over me with my tail.

Hmmmmmmmm!! Hmmmmmm!! Hmmmm!!!

Then a bright light starts flickering in front of my eyelids, making the darkness all pink.

The light just reminds me of the film crew in the sea yesterday. I put the pillow over my head.

"Come *hmmmmmm* on Harry. *Hmmmmm* it's time to *hmmmmmmmm* get up!" Humphrey, my humming-fish

alarm clock, is humming right in my ear. I'd been in such a bad mood last night I'd forgot to ask him not to wake me at the usual time.

"Leave me alone," I say from beneath the blankets.

"But it's time to rise and SHINE!" says Lenny, my lantern fish, shining his light right at my closed eyes again. He's swum under the blankets to point his light at me. Lenny and Humphrey are really useful when it comes to getting up in the morning, when you want to get up. But when you don't want to get up ever again they're a real pain.

"Look!" I shout, pushing back the blankets and roaring up out of the bed, "I'm not getting up!"

Humphrey *hmmmmms* quietly and Lenny flickers softly. Humphrey raises his fin. "I... I don't want to argue with you mate, but, you've umm... just got up."

He's right. I am out of bed.

Which is *exactly* what I didn't want to do.

Why does everything keep going wrong?

On top of that, I can hear someone coming down the corridor outside my bedroom. It'll be Mum, with a special breakfast to cheer me up.

I. Want. To. Scream.

As the door opens, I dart back into bed and signal to Humphrey and Lenny to be quiet with a dark look that makes them both shiver.

It is Mum, but she doesn't have breakfast.

"Morning angel-fish."

Humphrey and Lenny start sniggering behind their fins.

"I just wanted to tell you," Mum goes on, smoothing down the corners of my blanket, "Ralph and Joe have been knocking for you."

The last two people I want to see.

I groan.

Mum stops smoothing. "What's up, angel?"

I think quickly... then flop my fins out wide and stick out my tongue. Mum peers at it. I can see Humphrey and Lenny shaking their heads and hiding their faces in their fins. "I don't feel well." I say, flipping my tail slowly and painfully and doing a little cough.

Humphrey can't help himself and *hmmmms* in disgust, but I flick him a 'shut up' look from the other end of my hammer as mum places a fin on my

forehead to take my temperature.

"I don't think I can even swim to the kitchen for breakfast," I say, doing the little cough again.

"Well, you don't have a temperature," Mum says. "But if you don't feel well you'd better stay here, and I'll put the sea-cow steaks I had out for breakfast back in the fridge."

Sea-cow steaks?

My tummy grumbles at the thought. But I can't get out of it now. I groan and turn over in bed as Mum goes out saying, "Maybe Dad might want them in a sandwich to take to County Hall."

Today is shaping up to be as rubbish as yesterday and I haven't even left my room yet.

"Oi, Harry!" I hear Ralph from outside my bedroom window. "You getting up or what?"

Joe puts his tentacles through the gap in the window and unlocks the latch. The window opens wide and Ralph and Joe float in. Humphrey and Lenny float

out shaking their heads at me.

Joe hovers over the bed, counting something on his tentacles. "One, two, three, four, five, six," he counts out loud. "You do know that staying in bed all day is the seventh most dangerous thing to do in the world? What if there's a reefquake? You'll be tangled in your blankets and won't be able to get out. It's very, very dangerous staying in bed."

I push back the covers and sit up angrily. "I don't want to see anyone today. Not today, or for the rest of the holiday!"

Ralph and Joe look at each other.

"You're not still upset about

yesterday, are you?" Ralph asks.

"Yes Ralph, I am," I say, crossing my fins.

"Don't be silly," Ralph says with a smile. "Remember how we laughed at Joe when he got TWANGED off the seahorse in Shark Park? He didn't go all moody and say he didn't want to see anyone, did he?"

Well, no. He didn't.

"And," Ralph goes on, "what about when I went into the girls' loos by mistake on the first day of school? You and Joe laughed so much I thought you were going to explode. But I didn't get all

stupid and not talk to you, did I?"

No. He didn't.

I uncross my fins. A bit.

"Come on, Harry, it's only the second day of the holiday. We have a whole week to have fun. Let's forget about yesterday."

Ralph has a point. I completely uncross my fins and get out of bed.

"All right," I say. "But we aren't going anywhere near any cameras, okay?"

Within a couple of seconds we're out of the window and I'm calling to my mum in the kitchen as I swim past, "I'm going to the park with Ralph and Joe."

"But what about your cough?" Mum cries after me.

"It's much better, thanks."

"But what about your breakfast?"

"I don't want any."

"You haven't had any breakfast?" Ralph looks at me, panic-stricken.

"Nope. Sorry," I say.

"If this keeps up, I'm going to waste away! I'll shrink from a pilot fish into a pilchard and then where will you be?"

"I don't know."

"At the dentist with rotten teeth, that's where, because I won't have cleaned them for you."

"All right, all right," I say. "I'll have double helpings tomorrow, okay?"

Ralph thinks about this. "Okay, but I fancy seaweedabix, not prawn-flakes."

I sigh and nod. "Can we get going now, please?"

All this talk about food is making my tummy moan and grumble. I wish I hadn't pretended to be ill. I wish I'd got my teeth around Mum's sea-cow steaks!

When we get to the park we're the first on the swings. We even manage to get Joe to have a go.

Joe swings up high as Ralph pushes him and I swim in front, high-finning

Joe's tentacles as he comes close. But then Ralph gives one huge push and Joe is sent spinning right over the top of the swing, and flying straight towards me!

PLAP. PLAP. PLAP. PLAP. PLAP. PLAP PLAP. PLAP. PLAP PLAP. PLAP. PLAP PLAP. PLAP. PLAP PLAP. PLAP. PLAP PLAP. PLAP. PLAP.

...is the sound of Joe's tentacles

sticking to my hammerhead as Joe clings on for dear life and we fall back on to the seabed.

After that, the three of us are laughing so hard that I've completely forgotten about yesterday.

Except...

FLUBBERRRRRRRRRRRRRRRRRRRR!!!!

Suddenly, my stupid hammerhead is boinging all over the place and I can't see a thing as my eyes swivel and shake.

"Hello, Rubberhead!"

It's Rick.

He's sneaked up behind me and flubbered my head with his fin. Ralph and Joe catch hold of each end of my hammer to stop it shaking.

Donny, Cora and Pearl are there too, laughing at me as Rick circles around us. "Hey, it's Harry Hammerhead – the star of the funniest film of all time. Can't wait until that one HITS the

cinema!" laughs Rick. "It's going to be a
MASSIVE SMASH, just like it was on that
boat!"

Rick and Donny can hardly swim
upright they're laughing so much.

I'm about to tell Ralph and Joe that
we should go and leave those two idiots
to it, when suddenly something catches
my nose. Sharks have the best sense of
smell in the ocean and hammerheads
have some of the best senses of all of the
sharks, so I'm the first one to smell it.

It's a warm, fishy, tasty, yummy
smell and it's getting right in my nostrils.
I can feel it sliding right down my throat

and into my very empty tummy.

It is such a lovely smell. It doesn't just make my tummy rumble, it makes it almost shake with hunger – almost as if Rick has flubbered it!

I turn away from Rick towards the direction of the smell.

Rick is a bit put out by this. It's not the reaction he's expecting. He fins me on the shoulder. "Oi, don't turn away when I'm laughing at you!"

But I can't concentrate. The smell and the taste are beautiful, and my tummy is telling me to follow it, whatever Rick might be saying. I kick away and

use my shark sense to lock on to the
delicious aroma. I can dimly hear that
Rick is following me, telling anyone
who'll listen what a weirdo I am.

"Harry! Wait!" calls Ralph, but I
can't help myself. When a shark gets hold
of a scent, especially one as tasty as this,
there's no stopping them. I must find out
what it is, and I don't care what else is
happening!

I kick faster.

"Listen, Rubberhead, if you... oh...
oh... WHAT IS THAT SMELL?" Rick has
obviously caught scent of it too.

I kick even faster. Whatever it is, I

want to get to it first.

"H-H-H-Harry!!" calls Joe, "Don't go that way! It's towards the open o-o-o-ocean!"

But I'm not listening to Joe either. All I can hear is the grumbling in my tummy and all I can smell is the tasty scent.

"Come on Joe, we'd better follow them!" I hear Ralph calling to Joe, but I'm too far gone. I'm well out of the park now, swimming faster and faster. I can hear Rick talking as he kicks faster too. "That is the most delicious thing I've ever smelt," he says dreamily.

I kick harder. Rick is not getting there first.

Faster.

Faster.

I can feel the drool coming out of the corners of my mouth. I want that food, I want it now and I'm going to get it FIRST!

Faster!

FASTER!!

We're right off Shark Point now, out over the seaweed fields where the shepherd-fish tend their flocks. The scent is dragging us down into the forest of seaweed growing there. But it doesn't

slow me down. I kick on and I can feel Rick's breath on my tail.

He's closing.

FASTER!!!!

FASTER!!!!

In the dim distance, I can hear Ralph and Joe shouting, "Watch out!!! Harry, WATCH OUT!!!"

And then I can hear Donny shouting too. "RICK STOP! STOP!!!"

But the scent. It's too strong. I can't stop.

So as I burst between the thick fronds of seaweed, it's much too late to see that I'm heading straight towards

two wet-suited leggies, holding lights
and cameras while floating inside a huge
cage!

Rick and I are going too fast to stop!

We're going to crash right into
them!

Chapter 5

It's all a bit confusing what happens next – as you can see from the list that follows.

2.   WHAM! CRASH!
      TWAAAAAAANNNNGGGGG!!!

4.   I go bouncing and boinging off into the deep.

3. My hammerhead doesn't get stuck. For once.
1. We both put the breaks on, but we hit the cage at FULL SPEED!

See what I mean? Completely confusing.

I've bounced off the cage and am somersaulting through the water. I flap my fins, desperately trying to slow myself down. Eventually I get control over my body, but my head is a whole other problem! It's vibrating worse than when Rick flubbers it with his fin. I shake my head and try to stop the movement, and after a few seconds the ocean stops

rocking and I can start to make sense of what's happened.

The film crew have dropped a shark cage into the water and are filming from it. A shark cage isn't for catching sharks, it's to stop the leggies getting eaten by the sharks they're filming.

"Mmmmmmmmmmmmmmmmmmm!" For a moment, I think that Humphrey has followed me all the way from home, but then I realise it's me making that noise. I look down at my tummy and I remember how hungry I am. The smell of food that drew me and Rick here at full speed is almost too strong to bear. I turn on my

hammer-vision
and see that on
the seabed all
around the shark
cage, the leggies
have poured

buckets and buckets of juicy, yummy,
lovely shrimp!

They've obviously done it to get
sharks to appear, so me and Rick have
done exactly what they want. I don't care
though. Opening my mouth wide, I start
to swim about like crazy, shovelling in as
much shrimp as I possibly can.

It's the most amazing shrimp I've

ever tasted, and I honestly can't get enough. The delicious scent of it is in my nostrils, and the taste going all the way down from my mouth to my rapidly filling tummy is just mind-blowing.

In fact, I'm so busy concentrating on getting as much shrimp as possible that I almost don't realise that someone is calling for help.

Swallowing hard, I turn my hammer-vision back to normal, and see that Rick is caught in the bars of the cage!

The leggies seem delighted and are tickling him under the chin and

patting him on
the head as he
struggles to get
free.

"Help!
Help!" he sobs.
"Please get me
out of here!"

I can't help
having a little chuckle to myself, as I
shark down another mouthful of shrimp.
Poor Rick. I suppose I should help him
really, but then I notice that the film crew
are pointing their lights and cameras
right at me.

I feel my cheeks going red in embarrassment as I remember what happened yesterday and I start to cringe. I bet they're filming me because they're still making their film about comedy sharks, and I'm clearly the most side-splitting shark in the water.

I'm about to swim away and go and hide when I see the lady leggie reach down into the cage and take the lid off another fresh bucket of shrimp. She pours it into the water right in front of me, and then gives me a massive thumbs-up. She wants me to eat!

I dart forward into the cloud of tasty

shrimp and barrel-roll into a half fin-curl. The leggies applaud and lift their cameras and light up again. They want me to bust some more moves!

I don't need any more encouragement, and as I leap forward I have completely forgotten about yesterday and all the embarrassment. This is brilliant! I'm finally getting the chance to show everyone what I can really do. I power up over the cage, twisting into a radical ninety-degree hammer shift (the move only hammerheads can do, and the one I never do around Rick because it always makes him flubber me). The

leggies throw out even more shrimp as I turn that trick into a belly crunch and slide-swish right along the top of the cage.

"Harry! Harry! What about me?" calls Rick, still trying to get his head out from the bars.

I rub past Rick and tail-tickle him which drives the leggies crazy. They love it!

"Help! Help!" Rick cries.

"Har-ree! Har-ree!"

What?

I turn around, and I can't believe what I see. Not only have Ralph and Joe

and Donny arrived, but Cora and Pearl
have followed them out of the park, and
the dolphin twins are chanting my name!

Ralph and Joe are clapping along
as Cora and Pearl chant.

"Har-ree! Har-ree!!"

And I'm off again, swishing up past the cage. Using my hammer as an extra fin, so that I can turn quicker and tighter than any other shark, I twist into an ever-tighter spiral.

Building up speed.

Faster

Faster.

Just like yesterday. But this time I'm going to be heading down.

Faster!

FASTER!!!!

And then BANG!

With the sun above me lighting the water in an explosion of glittering

sparkles, I race down towards the cameras and the cage. I triple-gill, run three simultaneous back pikes and roll into a totally cool three-quarter gnash master. With a whoop and a yell I fall past the cage, do a complete body stall, a gnarly nose-endy, a floaty inside-outy that goes straight into a perfect outside-inny that Rick would have been over the moon to pull, and then, to finish off, using the edge of my hammer as a lever, I POP Rick right out of the bars out into the open water!

The leggies are going crazy. The light is on me, they're following my every

move with the camera and they're kicking their last buckets of shrimp into the water all around me.

I spin up, open-mouthed, through the shrimp, eating every bit.

As I turn back to the cage, I fold my fin across my now-full tummy and bow to the cage and the leggies inside. They've dropped their cameras and lights and are just applauding and cheering along with Ralph, Joe, Cora and Pearl.

Rick doesn't hang about. I can see from his cheeks that he is just as embarrassed as I was yesterday. He pulls Donny away from the group and heads

back towards Shark Point.

"Hey Rick," Pearl calls out as he slinks away, "bet you wish you were a hammerhead, don't you? That way your pointy head wouldn't have got stuck in the cage."

Cora giggles. "I can see how much you scared those leggies as well. They were so scared they could only tickle you under the chin!"

Soon Rick and Donny can no longer be seen.

And everyone else is laughing and cheering with me.

Except Ralph.

Ralph has prised open my mouth
and is eyeing all the bits of shrimp stuck
between my teeth.

"Breakfast at last!" he yells as he
dives in!

Chapter 6

Me, Ralph and Joe are just about the last Shark Pointers to get into the cinema tonight. It is absolutely packed.

We thread our way carefully between the rows, trying to get to our seats before the film starts. I ache all over from those moves I pulled for the

leggies in the shark cage earlier. It'll be a while before I do anything like that again, but it was a whole load of fun.

I have a humongous tub of shrimpopcorn, and Ralph's got two, having decided to take a night off eating stuff from between my teeth. I think this is more to do with the fact that Dad has finally given me my pocket money and I am paying!

Joe is too scared of the shrimpopcorn machine to get close enough to pick up a tub, so he had some, "Nice, safe ice-cream instead, not too cold though, because I don't want to get a frostbitten tentacle."

As we get to our seats I see that
Cora and Pearl are two rows in front of
us. They've got their aqua-phones on and
are seaberry messaging all their friends.
Cora catches sight of me, and fins Pearl,
who looks up. They both smile and wave.
Then they hold up their aqua-phones
and I see that they're not just messaging
their friends, they're posting pictures and
videos of me pulling all those stunts on to
Plaicebook!

I, of course, go red. But luckily, in the dim light of the cinema, no one knows except me.

Phew!

Girls.

I sit down between Joe and Ralph, just as the lights go down and the film begins.

WHAM!!!

Gregor is there on the screen, all huge and white and toothy. And pretty soon he's wrestling squids, and sword-fighting narwhales and racing to save the damselfish in distress.

It's great fun watching Gregor up

on the screen, and for a moment I think about my two days in front of the camera being a film star. Yeah, it was great for a short while, but when I think about my...

1. Aching fins (ouch)
2. Bruised hammer (ouchy)
3. All the flubbering Rick did with my hammery head (ouchy boingy)
4. Pictures of me appearing EVERYWHERE (cringey)
5. How tired I feel right now (zzzzz)

...all because of one small film I was accidentally in, I think that maybe I just don't have the energy to do it full time zzzzzzzzzz...

Ralph and Joe wake me up at the end of Parrotfish of the Caribbean.

As we swim back home, I realise that even though I don't want to be a world famous movie star any more, and even though I missed my hero Gregor's first ever movie, at least one brilliant thing has happened. This holiday hasn't been boring at all!

HARRY

Species:
hammerhead
shark
You'll spot him…
using his special
hammervision
Favourite thing: his
Gregor the Gnasher poster
Most likely to say:
"I wish I was a great white."
Most embarrassing moment: when Mum
called him her 'little starfish' in front of all his
friends

RALPH

Species: pilot fish

You'll spot him... eating the food from between Harry's teeth!

Favourite thing: shrimp Pop-Tarts

Most likely to say: "So Harry, what's for breakfast today?"

Most embarrassing moment: eating too much cake on Joe's birthday. His face was COVERED in pink plankton icing.

JOE

Species: jellyfish

You'll spot him… hiding behind Ralph and Harry, or behind his own tentacles

Favourite thing: his cave, as it's nice and safe

Most likely to say: "If we do this, we're going to end up as fish food…"

Most embarrassing moment: whenever his bum goes POP, which is when he's scared. Which is all the time.

RICK

Species: blacktip reef shark

You'll spot him... bullying smaller fish or showing off

Favourite thing: his black leather jacket

Most likely to say: "Last one there's a sea snail!"

Most embarrassing moment: none. Rick's far too cool to get embarrassed.

Coming soon...

More funny fishy tales
from Harry and the gang.

August 2013
ISBN: 978-1-84877-734-7

August 2013
ISBN: 978-1-84877-735-4

www.harry-hammer.co.uk

If you laughed at Harry, you'll laugh at these...

www.frogspell.co.uk

Out now
ISBN: 978-1-84877-139-0

Out now
ISBN: 978-1-84877-085-0

Out now
ISBN: 978-1-84877-711-8

Out now
ISBN: 978-1-84877-939-6

www.stinkyandjinks.blogspot.co.uk

Out now
ISBN: 978-1-84877-293-9

Out now
ISBN: 978-1-84877-294-6

July 2013
ISBN: 978-1-84877-295-3